For Amelia with love M.N.

For Amy S.L.

First published in Great Britain in 1998 by
Levinson Children's Books, a division of David and Charles Ltd.,
Winchester House, 259-269 Old Marylebone Road,
London NW1 5XJ

2 4 6 8 10 9 7 5 3 1 APR 3 0 2000

Text copyright © Margaret Nash 1998
Illustrations copyright © Stephen Lambert 1998

The rights of Margaret Nash and Stephen Lambert to be identified
as the author and illustrator of this work has been asserted by them
in accordance with the Copyright Designs and Patents Act 1988.

ISBN 1 899607 98 6

A CIP catalogue record for this title is available from the British Library.

Printed in Belgium

SECRET
in the MIST

Written by Margaret Nash

Illustrated by Stephen Lambert

LEVINSON BOOKS

Jonathan Quist had two secrets.

One was buried in a patch of sunny earth.

The other was buried in a patch of evening mist.

One morning Jonathan's mother opened the front door and saw something as thin as a pencil poking up from the patch of earth.

"What is that?" she asked.
"My secret," said Jonathan.
"My secret in the earth."

"A secret in a patch of earth,"
she said. "How wonderful."

Jonathan's mother smiled and shook
her duster so hard that golden dust
specks slithered into the sunshine.

One evening as Daddy was
closing Jonathan's bedroom curtains,
he looked into a patch of purple mist
and saw something silver glimmering
in the moonshine.

"What's that?" asked Daddy.
"That's my secret," said Jonathan.
"My secret in the mist."
"A secret in the mist," said Daddy.
"That's really something, Jonathan."

He tucked Jonathan
into bed and went
downstairs.

The secret in the patch of sunny earth
grew as tall as the watering can and it had
two little leaves like ears.

The secret in the mist grew as tall as the cat's proud tail and it waved in the night air.

The secret in the patch of earth
grew as high as the door handle.

Jonathan clapped his hands.

"Keep going," cried Jonathan. It did.

The secret in the patch of evening mist
grew as high as the window-sill.

All the moths and fireflies danced around it,
and a spider spun a glinting cobweb above it.

Both secrets grew and grew.

One was nudged by sunshine

and laced with summer rain.

The other lived in silver shadows
and was stroked by bright white moonlight.

"Taller, taller," Jonathan told them both.

They grew taller and taller and taller!

The secret in the patch of earth reached up to Jonathan's bedroom and tapped against the window-pane.

His sister Kate opened the window.

"Whatever is that thing?" she asked Jonathan.

"Not telling," said Jonathan.

The secret in the evening mist
swished against Jonathan's window
and lulled him to sleep.

Next morning when Jonathan looked out of his bedroom window, he saw his mother standing on the lawn. And his father and his sister Kate.

He saw the postman standing by the gate,

and the delivery man walking by.

They were all staring up at something...

Jonathan pulled on his clothes and rushed downstairs.
Towering above everyone was an amazing flower.

It was larger than the clock's round face,

bolder than the blackbird's song
and more golden than the sunshine.

"That's the flashiest flower I've ever seen," said his sister Kate.

Everyone cheered. And next door's dog barked for two whole minutes.

"That's the brightest secret I've ever seen,"
said his mother.
"A giant sunflower. It's magnificent."

Jonathan smiled and thought about his secret in the mist.

That night Jonathan climbed out of bed and crept
downstairs. Daddy came out of the sitting room
to see what he wanted.

Together they stepped out into the garden.
Above them stood a mysterious shape like a silver crown.
It glistened in the moonlight. No one cheered
but Daddy hugged Jonathan,
and Jonathan hugged Teddy.

"That's the most beautiful secret I've ever seen,"
said Daddy. "A giant moonflower. It's magical."

The moon slid silently behind a cloud.

Then suddenly . . . just for a second, the flower's grey stem turned green and the crown was tinged with gold.

"It's a sunflower by day
           and a moonflower by night,"
                              said Jonathan.

"So it is," said his parents. "How clever
of you to have made two secrets out of one!"